THE MYSTERIOUS VALENTINE

· Louanne Pig in ·
THE MYSTERIOUS VALENTINE

Nancy Carlson

Puffin Books

PUFFIN BOOKS
Viking Penguin Inc., 40 West 23rd Street, New York,
New York 10010, U.S.A.
Penguin Books Ltd, Harmondsworth, Middlesex, England
Penguin Books Australia Ltd, Ringwood, Victoria, Australia
Penguin Books Canada Limited, 2801 John Street, Markham, Ontario,
Canada L3R 1B4
Penguin Books (N.Z.) Ltd, 182–190 Wairau Road, Auckland 10,
New Zealand

First published by Carolrhoda Books, Inc., 1985
Published in Picture Puffins 1987
Reprinted 1987
Copyright © Nancy Carlson, 1985
All rights reserved
Set in Bookman

Manufactured in the U.S.A.
by Lake Book/Cuneo, Inc., Melrose Park, IL.

Library of Congress Cataloging in Publication Data
Carlson, Nancy L.   Louanne Pig in the mysterious valentine.
Reprint. Originally published: Minneapolis: Carolrhoda Books, © 1985.
Summary: When she receives a valentine from a
secret admirer, Louanne Pig tries to find out who sent it.
[1. Pigs—Fiction. 2. Valentines—Fiction] I. Title.
PZ7.C21665Lk 1987   [E]   86-16290   ISBN 0-14-050604-7

for sweethearts everywhere!!!

On February 14, Louanne looked in the mailbox and found the most beautiful valentine she'd ever seen. It was addressed to her!

Louanne raced inside.

"Look what I got!" she screamed. "A valentine from a secret admirer..."

I wonder who it's from."
"Eat your pancakes," said Dad.

On the way to school, Louanne showed her valentine to Harriet.

"Wow!" said Harriet. "That's the biggest valentine I've ever seen! Do you know who sent it?"

"Well, I know one thing about him," said Louanne. "He has a green pen. Look at the signature."

All through her math lesson, Louanne
thought about her valentine.

All through her geography lesson, she thought about the green pen. By the time her art lesson began, Louanne was determined to track down her secret admirer.

Maybe it's George, she thought. She peered over his shoulder. There was a blue pen on his desk, and a red pen too, and three chewed-up pencils. But there was no green pen.

"Hey, potato breath," said George, "quit breathing on me."

"Sorry," Louanne mumbled. She was glad it wasn't George.

Right before recess, Louanne got another
idea. It must be Arnie, she thought.

She waited until everyone else had left the
room. Then she crept over to Arnie's desk
and peeked inside. There were three crayons,
two paintbrushes, and five pencils sharpened
to perfect points—but no green pen.

"What do you think you're doing!" yelled Arnie from the doorway.

"Er...I needed a green pen," said Louanne.

"A likely story!" said Arnie. "You were probably after my candy bar." He grabbed the candy bar and marched out.

"I'm glad *you're* not my secret admirer," Louanne mumbled after him.

At lunch, Louanne checked Doug's pocket.
No green pen there.

That was just as well, she thought.

She checked Harold's book bag.

There was no green pen there either. That was a relief.

After school, she even asked Big Mike if *he* had a green pen.

"No way, pig!" he shouted at her. "What's it to you, anyway."

"Whew!" Louanne sighed as she made her escape. "I sure am glad it's not Big Mike!"

On her way home, Louanne stopped in at the card shop.

"Excuse me, sir," she said to the clerk. "You don't happen to remember who bought this valentine, do you?"

"I sure do," said the clerk. "He was a big
fellow with a curly tail."

"Do you remember his name?" Louanne asked excitedly.

"Sorry," said the clerk. "He never mentioned his name."

Louanne thought about the clerk's descrip-
tion all the way home. The trouble was, she
didn't *know* any big fellows with curly tails.

"I give up," she told her dad. "I can't figure out *who* sent me this valentine. All I can figure out is who I'm glad *didn't* send it."

"I guess it's just meant to be a mystery,"
said her dad.

"I guess so," said Louanne. "I wonder if
I'll get one next year."